Zodiac Spells

Teresa Moorey

Zodiac Spells

Illustrations by Cathy Brear

RYLAND

PETERS

& SMALL

LONDON NEW YORK

Senior Designer Sally Powell

Editor Miriam Hyslop

Picture Research Emily Westlake

Production Tamsin Curwood

Art Director Gabriella Le Grazie

Publishing Director Alison Starling

Editorial Consultant Christina Rodenbeck

First published in the United States
in 2003 by
Ryland Peters & Small, Inc.
519 Broadway, 5th Floor
New York NY 10012
www.rylandpeters.com

10 9 8 7 6 5 4 3 2 1

Text, design, and photographs
© Ryland Peters & Small, Inc. 2003

ISBN: 1 84172 514 5

Printed and bound in China.

contents

Did you realize that your star sign was the key to magic? One simple way to enchantment is to tap into the secret vibes of the zodiac.

how to use this book

But you don't have to restrict yourself to your own sign—develop the powers of the other signs by using their spells. Ever wished you were born under a different star? Get some of that Leo creativity and that Libra charm—and beat the Scorpios at their own game!

Find your own sign pages to discover your magical strengths, do your spell to maximize them—and then raid any sign you fancy.

Be a zodiacal all-rounder—and enjoy!

fire

aries leo sagittarius

aries
20 march—19 april

Powers of the Cosmos, brace yourselves! Aries' witch is on a mission, so no nonsense, please. Candles light almost by themselves, ignited by that fiery presence, and Aries' energy and willpower add tremendous voltage to rituals. Any lack of "finishiative" is more than made up for by bags of initiative, and Aries is an intrepid coven-leader for adventurous witches. Ram's confidence is a wonderful basis for magical success, but there can be no resting on laurels. Onward and upward—this broomstick is jet-propelled!

planet mars

day tuesday

element fire

trees gorse, hawthorn, larch

color red

stones ruby, bloodstone

incense or essential oils allspice, cumin, ginger, wormwood, dragon's blood

herbs pennyroyal, coriander

flowers and plants anemone, cacti

Use Aries energy for courage, enterprise, victory, and fantastic get-up-and-go.

aries victory spell

Aries are usually out in front—and rarely satisfied unless they are! These people have bags of fiery energy, but sometimes shoot themselves in the foot.

Aries: This spell will guarantee that Sign Number One is just that!

All signs: Plug into the Aries winning streak.

Light your candle and write what you want to win on the gingerroot with the pin. Imagine yourself winning—how wonderful it will be! Spread the powdered ginger on the plate and write your purpose in it with a fingertip.

Write your purpose on the paper with the red pen and either burn this in the candle's flame or attach it to the rocket, which you should ignite as you imagine your success. Watch it soar and explode in triumph! Let your candle burn down as far as possible.

Put a little of the powdered ginger in your clothing—for instance, in your shoes if you are running a race—and carry the root or place it nearby if possible—(for example, on your desk in a test).

The sky's the limit!

you will need:

a red candle and/or a firework, (preferably a rocket)

a piece of gingerroot

a pin

some powdered ginger

a plate (preferably red or orange)

some paper

a red pen

leo 23 july—22 august

It's a fact—Leos love to be the center of attention, and their flair for the dramatic means their friends can rely on them to make any ritual colorful—and fun. Making magic appeals to the Lion because it's a wonderful game. But the Big Cats' talents go deeper than plain showmanship. They are aware that a playful attitude is a creative one, and that when they relax and enjoy themselves, they are more in touch with the subtle realms. Besides, Leos are so generous (or bossy)—chances are they have no time for their own rites because they are too busy spelling them out for their pals!

planet sun

day sunday

element fire

trees walnut, juniper, cedar

color gold

stones diamond, carnelian, topaz, amber

incense or essential oils frankincense, sandalwood, orange

herbs chamomile, St. John's wort, rosemary

flowers carnation, marigold

Use Leo energy for charisma, self-belief, showmanship, and creativity.

leo creativity spell

Lions are very creative people, with many stylish and dramatic ideas, but even they can feel empty on occasion.

Leos: If you need a bit of extra oomph, try this spell.

All signs: Need an injection of inspiration? Read on for some Leonine flair.

Collect four pebbles—a dark pebble for practicality and concentration, bluish for clarity, red or gold for passion and energy, and green for calm and intuition.

This ritual is best done in sunlight. Heat the orange oil in your burner.

Draw an imaginary circle around you with your fingertip. Place the candle in the South of your circle. Place the dark pebble in the North, the blue in the East, the red in the South (with the candle), and the green in the West. Turn slowly clockwise, starting with North, asking for and visualizing the qualities of the pebble. Circle again, end facing South, and draw into yourself all the warmth and fire of the sun (or moon, or candle substitute). Let the glow fill your being, so you crackle with energy.

Circle clockwise, gathering the pebbles and placing them in the bag. Light the candle and keep the bag near you when you are being creative.

sagittarius

Saggie witch is on a quest. The Archer's more concerned with freeing the soul than little spells to make the garden grow, and friends get a buzz from the fiery inspiration. When the charcoal is damp and the spiral-dance turns into a knot, cheer-em-up Sag keeps the group smiling and spell-casting. That confidence gives any coven a boost, and the Archer's versatile mind quickly adapts tradition for the purposes of here-and-now magic. Sag has vision, and lights up the sky for others.

planet jupiter

day thursday

element fire

trees oak, maple, London plane

colors purple, magenta

stones amethyst, garnet

incense or essential oils agrimony, cinquefoil, clove, hyssop

herbs sage, meadowsweet, star anise

flowers honeysuckle, dandelion

Use Sagittarius energy for wisdom, long journeys, inspiration, prophecy, and anything that wants to "boldly go where no one has gone before."

This is a wise and deep-seeing sign, as the arrows of Sagittarean intuition take flight. But if they get it wrong, they may do so in a big way!

Sagittarius: Get Saggie savvy on target with this rite.

All signs: Notch-up your knowhow!

sagittarius wisdom spell

you will need:

a sage plant in a pot

a purple mug

some spring water

some purple cord or ribbon

a purple candle

Note: Sage may be dangerous during pregnancy.

Break three sage leaves from the plant and place them in the mug. Heat the spring water and pour it onto the leaves. Meanwhile, cut off enough sage sprigs to make a bracelet or chaplet. Wind them into shape using the purple ribbon—the result doesn't have to be neat.

Wearing your bracelet or chaplet, light the candle and sip your sage tea. Imagine your perspectives widening and inspiration coming to you as you watch the dancing candle flame.

earth

taurus virgo capricorn

taurus 20 april—20 may

This sensuous witch delights in the herbs and oils of magical craft. Gems, with their lustrous colors, appeal to Bulls, and that crystal ball gets gazed at simply for its beauty. Its value matters, too—money spells are Taurean favorites, with no silly qualms about doing workings for oneself! Taurus provides a grounding influence in the coven, but skipping around a midnight glade may not be quite the thing, unless the weather is balmy. Magic works best when it's comfy, and the rest of the coven agrees—especially when Taurus massages their over-stretched limbs with specially consecrated oil—aaah!

planet venus

day friday

element earth

trees peach, elder, cherry, apple

color green

stones emerald, lapis lazuli, jade

incense or essential oils cardamom, geranium, rose, vanilla

herbs thyme, catnip, wood sorrel, valerian

flowers daffodil, aster, columbine

Use Taurus energy for grounding, commitment, money, gardening, and anything that's about sheer enjoyment!

taurus commitment spell

Taureans love to commit and be committed to.
These reliable, down-to-earth folk like to know
where they stand.

Taurus: Use this spell to make sure your feet—and
everything else—stay on the ground.

All signs: This ritual will keep you as devoted as
a Bull to that important person or project.

Light your candle. Place the soil in the tray and bury your token under the surface. Put your fingers into the soil and feel its solidity and texture. Affirm that you are "planting" your commitment in solid earth.

Following the instructions on the packet, sow the seeds—if possible with a waxing moon. If this is for a relationship, why not sow them in a heart shape? Place the seeds somewhere dark to germinate and tend them carefully. Relight the candle whenever you need a reminder.

If the seeds don't grow? This shows you need more conviction. Just try again—once more, with FEELING!

you will need:

a brown candle (dark green will do if you can't find brown)

some soil

a seed tray

a symbol of the thing to which you're committing, for example a ring for a relationship, a key for a home

some small seeds

Burn incense containing thyme, if you wish

taurus money spell

Money is very important to this earth sign, for Bulls understand material values. But they love to spend on luxuries, too!

Taurus: This spell can boost your bank balance.

All signs: Swell your account and raise your interest! Decide on the exact sum you need before you start.

Light your candle and arrange your almonds around it. As you look at the flame, imagine clearly the arrival of the money (do not worry about where it may come from) and what you will do with it. Know that money is on its way; see it clearly.

Continue to visualize as you slowly eat the almonds. Now take the paper and green pen and write yourself a check/IOU for the money, clearly stating it is for you, NOW. Anoint this with a drop of almond or patchouli oil at each corner.

Place the check safely in your purse or wallet until real money comes to take its place. The money may come from several sources.

Spend it well!

you will need:

a green candle

some almonds
(inscribe multiples of $10
on the almonds with a pin to
make up your wished-for total)

a piece of paper

a green pen

some almond or patchouli oil

This spell is best with a waxing moon

virgo 23 august—22 september

A witch born under the sign of Virgo is an asset to any coven. She's probably a dab hand at writing rhymes, and she'll add a note of common sense to the proceedings. She's so reasonable that all the powers of the universe will willingly do her bidding. And when the rituals are over, she's happy to clean up when everyone else just wants to kick back and get their hands on the libation wine.

planet mercury

day wednesday

element earth

tree aspen, mulberry, pistachio

colors light green, pale yellow, muted colors

stones aventurine, agate

incense or essential oils lavender, bergamot, mace

herbs dill, fennel, lemon verbena, parsley

flowers and plants lily of the valley, clover, ferns

Use Virgo energy for healing, mental clarity, and concentration.

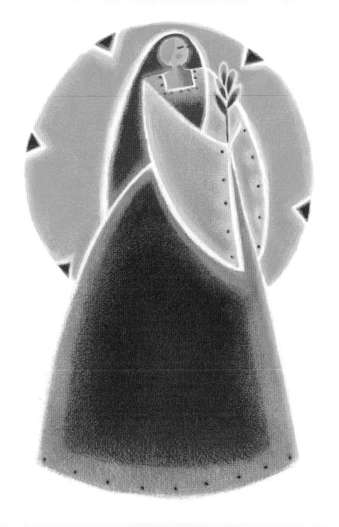

virgo healing spell

Because of their natural modesty, those born under the sixth sign of the Zodiac are often unaware that they may be blessed with the gift of healing.

Virgos: Use the healing spell to release your innate power.

All signs: Harness Virgo's energy with this spell to cure all ailments—from a broken heart to a broken limb.

Carve your initial, or that of the person you wish to heal, on the candle. Anoint the candle with some lavender oil and place the sprigs around it. Light the candle and say:

This candle I light, all ills take flight,
Soothing, healing, sweet balm feeling.

Chant this at least three times, and as you do so, imagine the sick or sad person healthy and vigorous (not "getting better"). If you are the sufferer, imagine a gentle green glow in the part of your body that's giving you problems. Breathe in the lavender fragrance and feel its gentle power.

The person who is not well should sleep with the lavender sprigs under their pillow, tied with a green ribbon.

you will need:
a green candle
some lavender oil
if possible, some lavender sprigs
a length of green ribbon

capricorn

Witchcraft is a serious business, and Cap studies the occult arts, determined to become a true magus. This witch would rather cast one small spell that works than get off a dozen flashy rites and have nothing to show but a hangover. The Goat likes to climb in the coven hierarchy and is only satisfied by becoming High Priest or Priestess. Everything is under control, from occult forces to scatty witches—and the matches are never forgotten!

planet saturn

day saturday

element earth

trees tamarisk, holly, elm

colors deep blue, deep green, black

stones onyx, apache tear

incense or essential oils patchouli, asphodel, bistort

herbs comfrey, fumitory, hemlock, hemp, mullein

flowers pansy, mimosa

Use Capricorn energy for matters to do with career, promotion, binding, grounding, building, and farming.

capricorn promotion spell

Goats are ambitious and competent, but may
not always be as self-possessed as they seem.

Capricorn: Who needs to power dress or go to
all those management seminars? Plug straight into
your unconscious and climb the corporate ladder
with confidence!

All signs: This is for you if you want to compete with
the Goats on the route onward and upward.

Do this spell when the moon is waxing to full—all the better if it falls on a Saturday. Anoint the candle with the patchouli oil, and as you rub it in, imagine yourself doing the job you want. Place a few drops also on the drawstring bag, the apache tear, and the job symbol. Light the candle and imagine again, really picturing yourself in the coveted post.

When you are ready, put the apache tear and symbol into the dark blue bag—your job is now "in the bag"!

Light your candle for a few minutes each day until full moon, and on the night before your interview. Take the apache tear with you to the interview. Congratulations!

you will need:

a dark blue candle

some patchouli oil

a dark blue drawstring bag

an apache tear (so much the better if it is set in a ring)

a symbol of the job you want—some office stationery, for instance

capricorn leadership spell

Caps often have the courage to make up their own minds, expecting others to follow. But occasionally they find they are alone.

Capricorn: Here is a spell for that extra something to put you out front.

All signs: Climb ahead with the best of the Goats!

Pick an effigy of your favorite god or goddess figure—choose an "all-round" deity such as Isis or Jupiter, to epitomize power. Place your effigy on a special shelf or altar, and beneath it place some of your hair and nail clippings.

Bring your deity flowers and offerings. Whenever you need a special boost to your leadership qualities, burn a joss-stick containing patchouli, asking for the power of the deity to be brought to earth, within you, and to make you a strong and wise leader.

Wave down from that mountaintop!

gemini libra aquarius

air

gemini

21 may—20 june

There's never a dull ritual with a lively Gemini witch in circle! Chants and spells spill out, and the altar's arranged and the censer swinging before you can say "Harry Potter"! Gem's inquiring mind explores as many magical systems as possible, but no theory is swallowed without being well chewed over—it has to be logical before it's magical. Twin witch understands the idea of "mirth with reverence," and that quick wit gets the whole coven giggling. A playful attitude can be a magical asset—as Gem knows instinctively!

planet mercury

day wednesday

element air

trees almond, ash, rowan

color yellow

stones agate, aventurine

incense or essential oils bergamot, lavender, lemongrass, mace

herbs parsley, marjoram, southernwood, mandrake

flowers and plants lily of the valley, fern

Use Gemini energy for communication, study, short journeys, and anything that requires being switched on and tuned in.

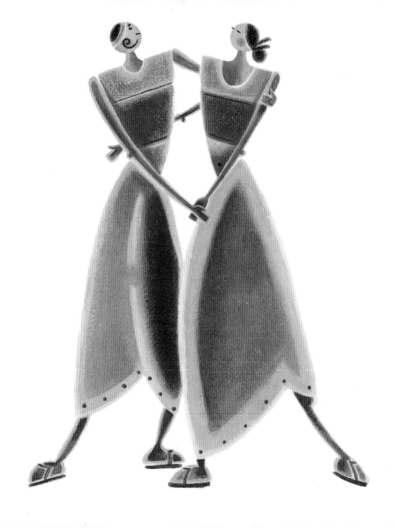

gemini communication

Gems are fab communicators, but even they
may sometimes find that although they are
talking, no one seems to be listening, or there
are hitches and delays with the mail,
deliveries, phone calls, and e-mail.

Gemini: The following will help
get the message through.

All signs: Plug in to some quick-thinking,
fast-talking Gemini vibes!

you will need:

a feather

a wind-borne seed

a small toy airplane, car, and train

*a piece of wire with a little
yellow clay at each end*

*a yellow drawstring bag, big
enough to hold the above*

some lavender oil

Leave all your objects out for a few hours in sunlight. When the moon is in her first quarter, put them in the bag. At full moon take out the oil and carefully anoint any equipment you have that's connected to communication—your phone, mail, computer, steering wheel, or stroke some on your throat to represent your vocal cords! If you are giving a talk, take your "medicine pouch" with you.

Store your lavender oil in the pouch to keep it charged up, and use as needed. Reboot it from time to time by leaving the contents out in the light of a waxing moon for an hour or so, before replacing in the bag.

Keep talking!

libra

23 september—22 october

Trust this witch to bring flowers for the altar, because a ritual means zilch unless it's a thing of beauty. And being nice costs nothing—after all, even the cosmic powers need a "please" and a "thank you." No wonder they eat out of that manicured hand! The coven runs all the smoother 'cos this witch is so keen on fairness and slick with diplomacy. When they want a spell to set up that love-fest or to look cool for a hot date, Libra's got it all sussed. But go easy on the eye of toad and wing of bat—this witch is a cut above all that!

planet venus

day friday

element air

tree birch, hornbeam, bramble, apricot

colors blue, pink

stones lapis lazuli, turquoise

incense or essential oils thyme, rose, alfalfa, geranium, orris, vervain

herbs balm of Gilead, coltsfoot, goldenrod

flowers primrose, violet, cowslip, cyclamen

Use Libra energy for harmony, love, understanding, justice, and a balanced outlook—and for all things beautiful!

libra harmony spell

Tactful Librans seem to radiate harmony and peace,
but strife upsets them.

Libra: This spell can help you to cast an aura
of calm all around.

All signs: You too can be surrounded by tranquility
and agreement with this ritual. It can also be used to
soothe just you alone.

Remember, this spell is NOT intended to influence
the life path of others, but merely to surround the
spell-caster with peace.

Light the candles and relax. Think of the most loving, pleasant, and gentle things that have happened to you. Allow yourself to smile and radiate gentleness. Pick up the lighted joss-stick and waft it around the bowl of candy, in time to your favorite soft music. Imagine love, peace, and blessing entering the candy.

Let the candles burn down, or keep them, wrapped carefully in blue cloth, in case you need to reboot the spell. Offer the candy to all concerned, or leave them on a table for people to help themselves. Fresh or dried fruit can be substituted for those on a diet. Dried apricots are ideal. Even a little wheat or rye bread will do.

You can use this spell simply for yourself, dedicating only food you choose to eat that has a fruity or sweet content.

A new and deeply nourishing way to comfort-eat!

libra love spell

Ruled by Venus, Libra is the sign of love. Librans are usually charming and affectionate, but they fear being alone.

Libra: Use this spell to boost your lovability.

All signs: Don't let Librans get all the attention! Grab yourself a piece of the action with this love spell.

Light the candles and the joss-stick (or heat the oil). Feel serene and peaceful with the world. Draw the symbol for Libra in the center of the card—a line with another line over the top that has a bubble in it (see page 40). Cut the card along the "bubbled" line.

It isn't hard to see which piece of card is "male" and which "female"! Dab your scent on the piece that fits your sex. On the other piece, list the qualities that you seek in a lover, being very careful not to describe a specific person (spells should never seek to influence another person directly).

Waft the pieces of card in the incense or oil vapor, and fit them back together like a jigsaw. Place them carefully inside your poetry book next to your favorite poem. Bring the two candles close together. Place the book somewhere safe and dream about the love that's coming into your life.

Thank you, Lady Venus!

you will need:

two pink candles

a rose joss-stick or rose oil for your burner

a piece of pink card

a pen

a pair of scissors

your favorite perfume or aftershave

a book of poetry

aquarius 20 january—17 february

The Water-Bearer likes spells that benefit humanity at large, so tree-planting ceremonies and peace rituals always appeal. Aquarius has the Kabbalah sussed and is the coven's resource for info on correspondences and magical symbolism of all sorts. This witch is ace at inventing rituals and is a cool spell-caster. Aquarius is a friend to all witches and can't be doing with any competition and pretension—who needs it? There are better things to do, like saving the world.

planet uranus

day saturday

element air

trees buckthorn, poplar, beech, ash

color electric blue

stones aquamarine, jet

incense or essential oils benzoin, mugwort, patchouli

herbs solomon's seal

flowers and plants mimosa, pansy, ivy, morning glory

Use Aquarius energy to bring change, to awaken life and surroundings, for idealistic causes, and anytime you want to put the cat among the pigeons!

Aquarians are great ones for lateral thinking, and may make abrupt changes. Strangely, they also resist change, especially if it isn't their idea.

Aquarius: Fling those perspectives even wider.

All signs: Get a fresh take on things and be unpredictable!

aquarius change

Burn the incense, light the candle, and put the socks on your feet. Think about what you want to change. Swap the socks from foot to foot, or turn them inside out. Slowly form the wire into any shape you feel like making. Let off the party popper and light the sparkler from one of the candles. Holding the sparkler, write *"Change for the better"* three times in the air. Let the sparkler burn out. Leave the candle to do the same, if you can, or relight it whenever you need waking up to change.

you will need:

incense containing benzoin

a bright blue or multicolored candle

socks in outrageous colors

a length of pliable thin wire

a party popper

an indoor sparkler

cancer scorpio pisces

water

cancer 21 june—22 july

Every coven needs a Cancer witch for a sense of family. Crab fusses over everyone's comfort and bubbles up something lush in the trusty cauldron. Crustacean instincts are spot on, and there are no problems deciding what magic to do, how to do it—and who to do it with! Crabby dreams are often stunning and explicit—this witch may wake up in the morning with a fabulous new ritual, brought straight from Otherworld. Home-loving enchanters perform plenty of spells to protect that precious pad—come in out of the cold into a haven of magic!

planet moon

day monday

element water

trees willow, lemon, eucalyptus

colors white, silver

stones sapphire, beryl, moonstone

incense or essential oils lemon balm, jasmine, calamus, camphor

herbs mallow, moonwort, loosestrife, chickweed

flowers lotus, lily, camellia, gardenia

Use Cancer energy for home and family, dreams, sea journeys, fertility, and anything to do with comfort and protection.

cancer fertility spell

Cancer is a sign with a talent for nurturing. Crabs are very maternal (or paternal), and they can have fertile imaginations too, but may use this negatively.

Cancer: This charm can also aid fertility of the mind. Just be clear before you start what you want to have fertilized!

All signs: Get some of that Cancerian power to make things grow.

Place the lilies on a sunny windowsill when the moon is waxing. For three mornings and three evenings, gently stroke off a little pollen with the feather, catching it very carefully in the eggcup. You only need a very little, and if you spill some, it doesn't matter—but watch out for the stains!

Place your eggcup between the two lighted white candles and imagine your fertility coming into being. Feel yourself blossoming, bringing a child of promise into the world, whether this is literal or metaphoric. Burn jasmine if you cannot smell the lilies.

Cover your eggcup with the cloth and place it beneath your bed to conceive, or next to your desk, easel, or piano for creative fertility. Relight the candles whenever you wish.

Go forth and multiply!

you will need:

*lilies growing in a pot
(stems in water will do)*

a feather

an eggcup

two white candles

a little jasmine oil or incense

a small piece of cheesecloth

cancer property spell

Crabs value their homes and are wonderful at creating an ambience of comfort and safety, although they may feel insecure sometimes.

Cancer: Keep all that you love safe with this spell.

All signs: Treasure what you value and make your own Crab's shell.

Starting at the top of your house, go around each room sprinkling salt and water, wafting the joss-stick, and carefully carrying the lighted candle. Say *"Be guarded by Earth"* with the salt, *"Be guarded by Water"* with the water, *"Be guarded by Air"* with the joss-stick, and *"Be guarded by Fire"* with the candle.

Next, go around the outside of your property the same way—a lantern will serve you better than an uncovered candle. Finally, "seal" your external doors and windows by passing the elements around them and asking for blessing.

you will need:
some salt
some water
a jasmine joss-stick
a white candle
a lantern or flashlight
a chalice
an incense cone
four cacti

Keep a chalice, a pot of salt, an incense cone, and a candle on a special shelf in your home, around a god/dess figure. Thus you have an altar with symbols of protection ever present.

Plant cacti around your house at each of the four quarters, or place them on windowsills. Sleep easy in your bed!

scorpio

23 october—21 november

This witch knows the true meaning of "occult." There's stuff that's just between Scorp and the subtle powers, and that's the way it'll stay! Scorpio has the nerve for a touch of the dark arts, with a store of black candles for the coven to raid for binding and banishing. Who needs to dance and chant when the power of the Scorpion's will alone is enough to send the spell into orbit? Kick back and relax, Buffy—the heavy mob's here now!

planet pluto

day tuesday

element water

trees yew, box, cypress, holly

colors black, wine red

stones tourmaline, bloodstone

incense or essential oils patchouli, wormwood, dragon's blood, asafoetida

herbs basil, nettle, sloe, thistle

flowers snapdragon, bryony, gentian

Use Scorpio energy for penetration, courage and endurance, passion, transformation, perception, concealment, and willpower.

scorpio lust spell

Steamy Scorpio knows all about being sexy.
These folk can be very magnetic, although
they can have trouble letting go.

Scorpio: Use this spell to make you even
more loved-up and uninhibited.

All signs: Turn yourself into a lust-bucket
to rival the Scorpio sizzle!

Heat enough wine for two with a leaf of basil and a drop or two of vanilla—do not let it boil. Decant this into two glasses for a lust-potion and leave them to cool.

After asking the plant, take a sprig of basil and wind it into a bunch with the red ribbon and a little of your hair. Add some of your own perfume, too. Hang it over the bed when you are going to make love. Place the basil plant on your bedroom windowsill.

Rub vanilla oil into the candles, and as you do so, imagine all the lovely, luscious things you're going to get up to when the candles are lit.

When the time is right, light the candles in your bedroom and place the wine where you and your lover can sip it.

Get ready for the earth to move!

you will need:

some red wine

a basil plant

some natural vanilla essence

a length of deep red ribbon

some vanilla oil

two wine-colored candles

pisces 18 february—19 march

Here we have a born witch—the material world gives Pisces far more trouble than the subtle planes! Fishes work magic instinctively, seeing spirits in the smoke and demons dancing in the candle flames—mind you, this could be because happy Fish has downed a bit too much of the sacred wine! Pisces' accepting ways and gentle intuition are balm to the coven, but sometimes this witch needs to be alone to make a special contract with the spirits— because sometimes it feels as if only they understand!

planet neptune

day thursday

element water

trees maple, ash, banyan, sweet chestnut

colors turquoise, purple, green

stones amethyst, alexandrite

incense or essential oils ylang ylang, clove, hyssop, nutmeg

herbs sage, anise, borage

flowers honeysuckle, dandelion

Use Pisces energy for intuition, imagination and empathy, meditation, and at any time you need to lose yourself in order to find yourself.

pisces insight

All Pisceans have a touch of the psychic, tuning in to what is unseen and unspoken, but are sometimes confused by it.

Pisces: Try the following to see clearly with your inner eye.

All signs: Get some Fishy foresight with this ritual.

A dark moon may be best for this ritual. Fill your bowl with water, light your candle, and make sure that its flame is reflected in the surface. Light your incense and, if you have one, crush a honeysuckle flower between your palms, rubbing the juice also on your third eye (the center of your forehead). If using oil, do the same.

Feel calm from the center down, and formulate your question. Take up the ink and let seven drops fall into the water. What shape/s do you see? They hold your answer! Gaze for as long as you like and make a note of your visions, even if they make no immediate sense.

You have the sight—use it wisely!

you will need:

a large bowl, preferably silver

a large silver candle

a little incense containing dried dandelion root and frankincense (if you can't cope with incense, a joss-stick of jasmine or frankincense will do)

some honeysuckle blooms if you can get them (or ylang ylang oil diluted in a carrier oil, two drops to a teaspoon)

some purple or green ink

index

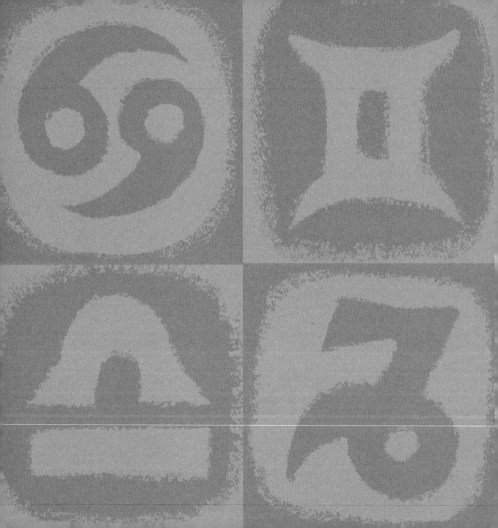